13579108642

Vintage
20 Vauxhall Bridge Road,
London SW1V 2SA

Vintage Classics is part of the Penguin Random House
group of companies whose addresses can be found at
global.penguinrandomhouse.com.

Joseph Anton was first published in the United Kingdom by Jonathan
Cape in 2012
Shame was first published in the United Kingdom by Jonathan Cape in 1983
Imaginary Homelands was first published in the United Kingdom by Granta
Books in association with Penguin Books Ltd in 1991
East, West was first published in the United Kingdom by Jonathan Cape in 1994
This short edition published by Vintage in 2017

penguin.co.uk/vintage

A CIP catalogue record for this book is available from the British Library

ISBN 9781784872687

Typeset in 9.5/14.5 pt FreightText Pro by Jouve (UK), Milton Keynes
Printed and bound by Clays Ltd, St Ives plc

Penguin Random House is committed to a sustainable future for
our business, our readers and our planet. This book is made from
Forest Stewardship Council® certified paper.

Home

SALMAN RUSHDIE

VINTAGE MINIS

From Salman Rushdie's memoir,
Joseph Anton

WHEN HE TURNED away from his father, wearing the blue-and- white-striped cap of Bradley House and the serge mackintosh, and plunged into his English life, the sin of *foreignness* was the first thing that was made plain to him. Until that point he had not thought of himself as anyone's Other. After Rugby School he never forgot the lesson he learned there: that there would always be people who just didn't like you, to whom you seemed as alien as little green men or the Slime from Outer Space, and there was no point trying to change their minds. Alienation: it was a lesson he relearned in more dramatic circumstances later on.

At an English boarding school in the early 1960s, he quickly discovered, there were three bad mistakes you could make, but if you made only two of the three you could be forgiven. The mistakes were: to be foreign; to be clever; and to be bad at games. At Rugby the foreign, clever boys who had a good time were also elegant cricketers or, in the case of one of his contemporaries, the Pakistani Zia Mahmood, so good at cards that he grew up to become one of the world's finest bridge players. The boys who had no sporting ability had to be careful not to be too clever and, if possible, not too foreign, which was the worst of the three mistakes.

He made all three mistakes. He was foreign, clever, non-*sportif*. And as a result his years were, for the most part, unhappy, though he did well academically and left Rugby with the abiding feeling of having been wonderfully well taught – with that nourishing memory of great teachers that, if we are lucky, we can carry with us for the rest of our lives. There was P. G. Lewis, known, inevitably, as 'Pig', who so inspired him with the love of French that he rose in the course of one term from the bottom to the top of the class, and there were his history teachers J. B. Hope-Simpson, aka 'Hope Stimulus', and J. W. 'Gut' Hele, thanks to whose skilled tutelage he was able to go on to win an exhibition, a minor scholarship, to read history at his father's old alma mater, King's College, Cambridge, where he would meet E. M. Forster and discover sex, though not at the same time. (Less valuably, perhaps, 'Hope Stimulus' was also the person who introduced him to Tolkien's *The Lord of the Rings*, which entered his consciousness like a disease, an infection he never managed to shake off.) His old English teacher Geoffrey Helliwell would be seen on British television on the day after the fatwa, ruefully shaking his head and asking, in sweet, vague, daffy tones,

'Who'd have thought such a nice, quiet boy could get into so much trouble?'

Nobody had forced him to go to boarding school in England. Negin had been against the idea of sending her only son away across oceans and continents. Anis had offered him the opportunity and encouraged him to take the Common Entrance exam, but, even after he came through that with some distinction and the place at Rugby was his, the final decision to go or stay was left entirely to him. In later life he would wonder at the choice made by this thirteen-year-old self, a boy rooted in his city, happy in his friends, having a good time at school (apart from a little local difficulty with the Marathi language), the apple of his parents' eye. Why did that boy decide to leave it all behind and travel halfway across the world into the unknown, far from everyone who loved him and everything he knew? Was it the fault, perhaps, of literature (for he was certainly a bookworm)? In which case the guilty parties might have been his beloved Jeeves and Bertie, or possibly the Earl of Emsworth and his mighty sow, the Empress of Blandings. Or might it have been the dubious attractions of the world of Agatha Christie that persuaded him, even if Christie's Miss Marple made her home in the most murderous village in England, the lethal St Mary Mead? Then there was Arthur Ransome's *Swallows and Amazons* series telling of children messing about in boats in the Lake District, and, much, much worse, the terrible literary escapades of Billy Bunter, the 'Owl of the Remove',

Why did that boy decide to leave it all behind and travel halfway across the world into the unknown?

the fat boy at Frank Richards's ridiculous Greyfriars
School, where, among Bunter's classmates, there was at
least one Indian, Hurree Jamset Ram Singh, the 'dusky
nabob of Bhanipur', who spoke a bizarre, grand, syntacti-
cally contorted English ('the contortfulness', as the dusky
nabob might well have put it, 'was terrific'). Was it, in
other words, a *childish* decision, to venture forth into an
imaginary England that only existed in books? Or was it,
alternatively, an indication that beneath the surface of the
'nice, quiet boy' there lurked a stranger being, a fellow with
an unusually adventurous heart, possessed of enough
gumption to take a leap in the dark exactly *because* it was a
step into the unknown – a youth who intuited his future
adult self's ability to survive, even to thrive, wherever in
the world his wanderings might take him, and who was
able, too easily, even a little ruthlessly, to follow the dream
of 'away', breaking away from the lure, which was also, of
course, the tedium, of 'home', leaving his sorrowing
mother and sisters behind without too much regret? Perhaps a little of each. At any rate, he took the leap, and the
forking paths of time bifurcated at his feet. He took the
westward road and ceased to be who he might have been if
he had stayed at home.

A pink stone set into the Doctor's Wall, named for the
legendary headmaster Dr Arnold and overlooking the storeyed playing fields of the Close, bore an inscription that
purported to celebrate an act of revolutionary iconoclasm.
'This is to commemorate the exploit of William Webb

Ellis,' it read, 'who, with a fine disregard for the rules of football as played in his time, first picked up the ball and ran with it, thus originating the distinctive feature of the rugby game.' But the Webb Ellis story was apocryphal, and the school was anything but iconoclastic. The sons of stockbrokers and solicitors were being educated here and 'a fine disregard for the rules' was not on the curriculum. Putting both your hands in your pockets was against the rules. So was 'running in the corridors'. However, fagging – acting as an older boy's unpaid servant – and beating were still permitted. Corporal punishment could be administered by the housemaster or even by the boy named as Head of House. In his first term the Head of House was a certain R. A. C. Williamson who kept his cane hanging in full view over the door of his study. There were notches in it, one for each thrashing Williamson had handed out.

He was never beaten. He was a 'nice, quiet boy'. He learned the rules and observed them scrupulously. He learned the school slang, *dics* for bedtime prayers in the dormitories (from the Latin *dicere*, to speak), *topos* for the toilets (from the Greek word for *place*), and, rudely, *oiks* for non-Rugby School inhabitants of the town, a place best known for the manufacture of cement. Though the Three Mistakes were never forgiven, he did his best to fit in. In the sixth form he won the Queen's Medal for a history essay about Napoleon's foreign minister, the clubfooted, cynical, amoral libertine Talleyrand, whom he vigorously defended. He became secretary of the school's debating society and spoke eloquently in favour of fagging, which was abolished not long after his schooldays ended. He came from a conservative Indian family and was in no sense a radical. But racism was something he quickly understood. When he returned to his little study, he more than once found an essay he had written torn to pieces, which were scattered on the seat of his red armchair. Once somebody wrote the words WOGS GO HOME on his wall. He gritted his teeth, swallowed the insults and did his work. He did not tell his parents what school had been like until after he left it (and when he did tell them they were horrified that he had kept so much pain to himself). His mother was suffering because of his absence, his father was paying a fortune for him to be there, and it would not be right, he told himself, to complain. So in his letters home he created his first fictions, about idyllic schooldays of sunshine and cricket. In fact he was no good at cricket and Rugby in winter was bitterly cold, doubly so for a boy from the tropics who had never slept under heavy blankets and found it hard to go to sleep when so weighed down. But if he cast them off, then he shivered. He had to get used to this weight also, and he did. At night in the dormitories, after lights out, the metal-frame beds began to shake as the boys relieved their adolescent urges, and the banging of the beds against the heating pipes running around the walls filled the large dark rooms with the night music of inexpressible desire. In this matter, as in all else, he strove to be like the others, and join in. Again: he was not, by nature, rebellious. In those early days, he preferred the Rolling Stones to the Beatles, and, after one of his friendlier housemates, a serious, cherubic boy named Richard Shearer, made him sit down and listen to *The Free-wheelin' Bob Dylan*, he became an enthusiastic Dylan worshipper; but he was, at heart, a conformist.

Still: almost as soon as he came to Rugby he did rebel. The school insisted that all boys should enrol in the CCF, or Combined Cadet Force, and then climb into full military khaki on Wednesday afternoons to play war games in the mud. He was not the sort of boy who thought that might be fun – indeed, it struck him as a kind of torture – and in the first week of his school career he went to see his housemaster, Dr George Dazeley, a mild-natured mad-scientist type with a glittering, mirthless smile, to explain to him that he did not wish to join. Dr Dazeley stiffened, glittered and pointed out, just a little icily, that boys did not have the right to opt out. The boy from Bombay, suddenly possessed by an unaccustomed stubbornness, drew himself up straight. 'Sir,' he said, 'my parents' generation have only recently fought a war of liberation against the British Empire, and therefore I cannot possibly agree to join its armed forces.' This unexpected burst of post-colonial passion stymied Dr Dazeley, who limply gave in and said, 'Oh, very well, then you'd better stay in your study and read instead.' As the young conscientious objector left his office Dazeley pointed to a picture on the wall. 'That is Major William Hodson,' he said. 'Hodson of Hodson's Horse. He was a Bradley boy.' William Hodson was the British cavalry officer who, after the suppression of the Indian Uprising of 1857 (at Rugby it was called *the Indian Mutiny*), captured the last Mughal emperor, the poet Bahadur Shah Zafar, and murdered his three sons, stripping them naked, shooting them dead, taking their jewellery, and throwing their bodies down in the dirt at one of the gates of Delhi, which was thereafter known as the Khooni Darvaza, the gate of blood. That Hodson was a former Bradley House resident made the young Indian rebel even prouder of having refused to join the army in which the executioner of the Mughal princes had served. Dr Dazeley added, vaguely, and perhaps incorrectly, that he believed Hodson had been one of the models for the character of Flashman, the school bully in Thomas Hughes's novel of Rugby, *Tom Brown's Schooldays*. There was a statue of Hughes on the lawn outside the school library, but here at Bradley House the presiding old-timer was the alleged real-life original version of the most famous bully in English literature. That seemed just about right.

The lessons one learns at school are not always the ones the school thinks it's teaching.

For the next four years he spent Wednesday afternoons reading yellow-jacketed science-fiction novels borrowed from the town library, while eating egg-salad sandwiches and crisps, drinking Coca-Cola and listening to *Two-Way Family Favourites* on the transistor radio. He became an expert on the so-called golden age of science fiction, devouring such masterworks as Isaac Asimov's *I, Robot*, wherein the Three Laws of Robotics were enshrined, Philip K. Dick's *The Three Stigmata of Palmer Eldritch*, Zenna Henderson's *Pilgrimage* novels, the wild fantasies of L. Sprague de Camp, and, above all, Arthur C. Clarke's haunting short story 'The Nine Billion Names of God', about the world quietly coming to an end once its secret purpose, the listing of all God's names, had been fulfilled by a bunch of Buddhist monks with a supercomputer. (Like his father, he was fascinated by God, even if religion held little appeal.) It might not have been the greatest revolution in history, this four-and-a-half-year fall towards the fantastic fuelled by tuckshop snack foods, but every time he saw his schoolfellows come lurching in from their war games, exhausted, muddy and bruised, he was reminded that standing up for oneself could sometimes be well worth it.

In the matter of God: the last traces of belief were erased from his mind by his powerful dislike of the architecture of Rugby Chapel. Many years later, when by chance he passed through the town, he was shocked to find that Herbert Butterfield's neo-Gothic building was in fact extremely beautiful. As a schoolboy he thought it hideous, deciding, in that science-fiction-heavy time of his life, that it resembled nothing so much as a brick rocket ship ready for take-off; and one day when he was staring at it through the window of a classroom in the New Big School during a Latin lesson, a question occurred. 'What kind of God,' he wondered, 'would live in a house as ugly as that?' An instant later the answer presented itself: obviously no self-respecting God would live there – in fact, obviously, there *was* no God, not even a God with bad taste in architecture. By the end of the Latin lesson he was a hard-line atheist, and to prove it, he marched determinedly into the school tuckshop during break and bought himself a ham sandwich. The flesh of the swine passed his lips for the first time that day, and the failure of the Almighty to strike him dead with a thunderbolt proved to him what he had long suspected: that there was nobody up there with thunderbolts to hurl.

Inside Rugby Chapel he joined the rest of the school, one term, in rehearsing and singing the Hallelujah Chorus as part of a performance of the full *Messiah* with professional soloists. He took part in compulsory matins and evensong – having attended the Cathedral School in Bombay, he had no leg to stand on if he wanted to make an argument that would excuse him from mumbling his way through Christian prayers – and he couldn't deny that he liked the hymns, whose music lifted his heart. Not all the hymns; he didn't, for example, need to *survey the wondrous cross / on which the prince of glory died*; but a lonely boy could not help but be touched when he was asked to sing *The night is dark and I am far from home / Lead Thou me on*. He liked singing 'O Come, All Ye Faithful' in Latin, which somehow took the religious sting out of it: *venite, venite in Bethlehem*. He liked 'Abide with Me' because it was sung by the whole 100,000-strong crowd at Wembley Stadium before the FA Cup Final, and what he thought of as the 'geography hymn', 'The Day Thou Gavest, Lord, Is Ended', made him sweetly homesick: *The sun that bids us rest is waking / our brethren 'neath the western* [here he would substitute *eastern*] *sky.* The language of unbelief was distinctly poorer than that of belief. But at least the music of unbelief was becoming fully the equal of the songs of the faithful, and as he moved through his teenage years and the golden age of rock music filled his ears with its pet sounds, its I-can't-get-no and hard rain and try-to-see-it-my-way and da doo ron ron, even the hymns lost some of their power to move him. But there were still things in Rugby Chapel to touch a bookish unbeliever's heart: the memorials to Matthew Arnold and his ignorant armies clashing by night, and Rupert Brooke, killed by a mosquito bite while fighting just such an army, lying in some corner of a foreign field that was forever England; and, above all, the stone in memory of Lewis Carroll, with its Tenniel silhouettes dancing around the edges in black-and-white marble in a – why, a kind of – yes! – quadrille. 'Would not, could not, would not, could not, would not join the dance,' he sang softly to himself. 'Would not, could not, would not, could not, could not join the dance.' It was his private hymn to himself.

Before he left Rugby he did a terrible thing. All school leavers were allowed to hold a 'study sale', which allowed them to pass on their old desks, lamps and other bric-a-brac to younger boys in return for small amounts of cash. He posted an auction sheet on the inside of his study door, stipulated modest starting prices for his redundant possessions, and waited. Most study-sale items were heavily worn; he, however, had his red armchair, which had been new when his father bought it for him. An armchair with only one user was a high-quality, sought-after rarity in the study-sales and the red chair attracted some serious bidding. In the end there were two energetic bidders: one of his fags, a certain P. A. F. Reed-Herbert, known as 'Weed Herbert', a small, bespectacled little worm of a fellow who hero-worshipped him a little, and an older boy named John Tallon, whose home was on The Bishop's Avenue, the millionaires' row of north London, and who could presumably afford to bid high.

When the bidding slowed down – the top bid was Reed-Herbert's offer of around five pounds – he had his terrible idea. He secretly asked John Tallon to post a seriously high bid, something like *eight pounds*, and promised him that he would not hold him to it if that ended up as the highest offer. Then, at *dics*, he told Weed Herbert solemnly that he knew for a fact that his wealthy rival, Tallon, was prepared to go even higher, perhaps even as high as twelve whole pounds. He saw Weed Herbert's face fall, noted his crushed expression and went in for the kill. 'Now, if you were to offer me, say, ten quid right away, I could close the auction and declare the chair sold.' Weed Herbert looked nervous. 'That's a lot of money, Rushdie,' he said. 'Think about it,' said Rushdie magnanimously, 'while you say your prayers.'

When *dics* were over, Weed Herbert took the bait. The Machiavellian Rushdie smiled reassuringly. 'Excellent decision, Reed-Herbert.' He had cold-bloodedly persuaded the boy to bid against himself, doubling his own top bid. The red armchair had a new owner. Such was the power of prayer.

This happened in the spring of 1965. Nine and a half years later, during the general election campaign of October 1974, he turned on his television set and saw the end of a speech by the candidate for the far-right, racist, fascist, vehemently anti-immigrant British National Front. The candidate's name was titled on the screen. *Anthony Reed-Herbert.* 'Weed Herbert!' he cried aloud in horror. 'My God, I've invented a Nazi!' It all instantly became plain. Weed Herbert, tricked into spending too much of his own money by a conniving, godless wog, had nursed his bitter rage through wormy childhood into wormier adulthood and had become a racist politician so that he could be revenged upon all wogs, with or without overpriced red armchairs to sell. (But was it the same Weed Herbert? Could there possibly have been two of them? No, he thought, it had to be little P. A. F., little no more.) In the 1974 election Weed Herbert received 6 per cent of the vote in the Leicester East constituency, 2,967 votes in all. In August 1977 he ran again, in the Birmingham Ladywood by-election, and came in third, ahead of the Liberal candidate. Mercifully that was his last significant appearance on the national scene.

Mea culpa, thought the vendor of the red armchair. *Mea maxima culpa.* In the true story of his schooldays there would always be much loneliness and some sadness. But there would also be this stain on his character; this unrecorded, unexpiated crime.

ON HIS SECOND day at Cambridge he went to a gathering of freshmen in King's College Hall and gazed for the first time upon the great Brunelleschian dome of Noel Annan's head. Lord Annan, provost of King's, the sonorous cathedral of a man whose dome that was, stood before him in all his cold-eyed, plump-lipped glory. 'You are here,' Annan told the assembled freshmen, 'for three reasons: Intellect! Intellect! Intellect!' One, two, three fingers stabbed the air as he counted off the three reasons. Later in his speech he surpassed even that aperçu. 'The most important part of your education here will not take place in the lecture rooms or libraries or supervisions,' he intoned. 'It will happen when you sit in one another's rooms, late at night, fertilising one another.'

He had left home in the middle of a war, the pointless India–Pakistan conflict of September 1965. The eternal bone of contention, Kashmir, had triggered a five-week war in which almost seven thousand soldiers died, and at the end of which India had acquired an extra seven hundred square miles of Pakistani territory, while Pakistan had seized two hundred square miles of Indian land, and nothing, less than nothing, had been achieved. (In *Midnight's*

Children, this would be the war in which most of Saleem's family is killed by falling bombs.) For some days he had stayed with distant relatives in London in a room without a window. It was impossible to get through to his family on the telephone, and telegrams from home, he was told, were taking three weeks to get through. He had no way of knowing how everyone was. All he could do was to catch the train to Cambridge, and hope. He arrived at King's College's Market Hostel in bad shape, exacerbated by his fear that the university years ahead would be a repeat of the largely wretched Rugby years. He had pleaded with his father not to send him to Cambridge, even though he had already won his place. He didn't want to go back to England, he said, to spend more years of his life among all those cold, unfriendly fish. Couldn't he stay home and go to college among warmer-blooded creatures? But Anis persuaded him to go. And then told him he had to change his subject of study. History was a useless thing to waste three years on. He had to tell the college he wanted to switch to economics. There was even a threat: if he didn't do that, Anis would not pay his fees.

Burdened by three fears of unfriendly English youth, of economics and of war – he found, on his first day up at King's, that he couldn't get out of bed. His body felt heavier than usual, as if gravity itself were trying to hold him back. More down than up, he ignored several knocks on the door of his somewhat Scandinavian-modern room. (It was the year of the Beatles' *Rubber Soul*, and he spent a good deal of it humming 'Norwegian Wood'.) But in the early evening a particularly insistent pounding forced him out of bed. At the door wearing a huge Old Etonian grin and Rupert Brooke's wavy blond hair was the tall, relentlessly friendly figure of 'Jan Pilkington-Miksa – I'm half-Polish, you know', the welcoming angel at the gateway to the future, who brought him forth on a tide of loud bonhomie into his new life.

Jan Pilkington-Miksa, the very platonic form of the English public schoolboy, looked exactly like all the creatures at Rugby who had made his life so unpleasant, but he was the sweetest-natured of young men, and seemed to have been sent as a sign that things were going to be different this time round. And so they were; Cambridge largely healed the wounds that Rugby had inflicted, and showed him that there were other, more attractive Englands to inhabit, in which he could easily feel at home.

So much for the first burden. As for economics, he was rescued by a second welcoming angel, the director of studies, Dr John Broadbent, an Eng. Lit. don so magnificently groovy that he could easily have been (though he was not) one of the models for the supercool and ultra-permissive Dr Howard Kirk, hero of Malcolm Bradbury's novel *The History Man*. Dr Broadbent asked him, when he gloomily said that he was supposed to change subjects because his father insisted on it, 'And what do *you* want to do?' Well, he didn't want to read economics, obviously; he had a history exhibition and he wanted to read history. 'Leave it to me,'

Dr Broadbent said, and wrote Anis Rushdie a gentle but fierce letter stating that in the opinion of the college Anis's son Salman was not qualified to read economics and that if he continued to insist upon doing so it would be better to remove him from the university to make room for someone else. Anis Rushdie never mentioned economics again.

The third burden, too, was soon lifted. The war in the subcontinent ended, and everyone he loved was safe. His university life began.

He did the usual things: made friends, lost his virginity, learned how to play the mysterious matchstick game featured in *L'année dernière à Marienbad*, played a melancholy game of croquet with E. M. Forster on the day Evelyn Waugh died, slowly understood the meaning of the word 'Vietnam', became less conservative, and was elected to the Footlights, became a minor bulb in that dazzling group of illuminati – Clive James, Rob Buckman, Germaine Greer – and watched Germaine perform her Stripping Nun routine, bumping and grinding her way out of her sisterly habit to reveal a full frogman's outfit beneath, on the tiny club stage in Petty Cury on the floor below the office of the Chinese Red Guards where Chairman Mao's Little Red Book was on sale. He also inhaled, saw one friend die of bad acid in the room across the hall, saw another succumb to drug-induced brain damage, was introduced to Captain Beefheart and the Velvet Underground by a third friend who died soon after they graduated; enjoyed miniskirts and see-through blouses; wrote briefly for the student paper *Varsity* until it decided it didn't need his services; acted in Brecht, Ionesco and Ben Jonson; and crashed Trinity May Ball with the future art critic of *The Times* to listen to Françoise Hardy sing the anthem of young loveless anguish, 'Tous les garçons et les filles'.

In later life he often spoke of the happiness of his Cambridge years, and agreed with himself to forget the hours of howling loneliness when he sat alone in a room and wept, even if King's Chapel was right outside his window blazing with beauty (this was in his final year, when he was living on the ground floor of S staircase in the college itself, in a room with a view, if ever there was one – chapel, lawn, river, punts – a cliché of gorgeousness). In that final year he had returned from the holidays in low spirits. That was at the end of the summer of 1967, the Summer of Love, when, if you were going to San Francisco, you had to be sure to wear some flowers in your hair. He, unfortunately, had been in London with nobody to love. By chance he had found himself at the very heart of 'where', in the parlance of those days, 'it was at', staying in a rented room above the coolest boutique of all, Granny Takes a Trip, at the World's End end of the King's Road. John Lennon's wife Cynthia wore the frocks. *Mick Jagger* was rumoured to wear the frocks.

Here, too, there was an education to be had. He learned not to say 'fab' or 'groovy'. At Granny's, you said 'beautiful' to express mild approval, and, when you wanted to call something beautiful, you said 'really nice'. He got used to nodding his head a lot, wisely. In the quest for cool, it helped that he was Indian. 'India, man,' people said. 'Far out.' 'Yeah,' he said, nodding. 'Yeah.' 'The Maharishi, man,' people said. 'Beautiful.' 'Ravi Shankar, man,' he replied. At this point people usually ran out of Indians to talk about and everyone just went on nodding, beatifically. 'Right, right,' everyone said. 'Right.'

He learned an even more profound lesson from the girl who ran the shop, an ethereal presence sitting in that fashionably darkened, patchouli-oil-scented space heavy with sitar music, in which, after a time, he became aware of a low purple glow, in which he could make out a few motionless shapes. These were probably clothes, probably for sale. He didn't like to ask. Granny's was frightening. But one day he plucked up his courage and went downstairs to introduce himself, *Hi, I'm living upstairs, I'm Salman.* The girl in the shop came close, so that he could see the contempt on her face. Then slowly, fashionably, she shrugged.

'Conversation's dead, man,' she said.

Up and down the King's Road walked the most beautiful girls in the world, ridiculously underdressed, accompanied by peacocking men who were equally ridiculously overdressed, in high-collared frock coats and frilly shirts and flared crushed velvet trousers and fake-snakeskin boots. He seemed to be the only one who didn't know what it was to be happy.

He returned to Cambridge feeling, at the ripe old age of

twenty, that life was passing him by. (Others had the final-year blues, too. Even the invariably cheerful Jan Pilkington-Miksa was deeply depressed; though happily he did recover to declare that he had decided to be a film director, and intended to head for the south of France as soon as he was done with Cambridge, 'because', he said airily, 'they probably need film directors down there'.) He took refuge in work, just as he had at Rugby. *The intellect of man is forced to choose | Perfection of the life or of the work*, Yeats said, and since the perfect life was plainly beyond him he had better look to the work instead.

That was the year he found out about the satanic verses. In Part Two of the History Tripos he was expected to choose three 'special subjects' from a wide selection on offer, and concentrate on those. He chose to work on Indian history during the period of the independence struggle against the British, from the 1857 uprising to Independence Day in August 1947; and the extraordinary first century or so of the history of the United States, 1776–1877, from the Declaration of Independence to the end of the post-Civil War period known as Reconstruction; and a third subject, offered, that year, for the first time, titled 'Muhammad, the Rise of Islam and the Early Caliphate'. In 1967 few history students at Cambridge were interested in the Prophet of Islam – so few, in fact, that the course's designated lecturer cancelled his proposed lectures and declined to supervise the few students who had chosen the course. This was a way of saying that the subject was no longer available, and another choice should be made. All the other students did indeed abandon the Muhammad paper and go elsewhere. He, however, felt an old stubbornness rise in him. If the subject was offered, it could not be cancelled as long as there was a single student who wished to study it; that was the rule. Well, he did want to study it. He was his father's son, godless, but fascinated by gods and prophets. He was also a product, at least in part, of the deep-rooted Muslim culture of South Asia, the inheritor of the artistic, literary and architectural riches of the Mughals and their predecessors. He was determined to study this subject. All he needed was a historian who was willing to supervise him.

Of the three great historians who were fellows of King's at that time, Christopher Morris was the most published, with the most established reputation, historian of Tudor political thought, ecclesiastical history and the Enlightenment, while John Saltmarsh was one of the grand eccentrics of the university with his wild white hair, muttonchop side whiskers, long-john underwear poking out at his trouser cuffs above his sockless, sandalled feet, the unrivalled expert in the history of the college and chapel, and, more broadly, in the local history of the region, often seen tramping the country lanes around Cambridge with a rucksack on his back. Both Morris and Saltmarsh were disciples of Sir John Clapham, the scholar who established economic history as a serious field of study, and both conceded that the third member of the King's history trinity,

Arthur Hibbert, a medievalist, was the most brilliant of them all, a genius who, according to college legend, had answered the questions he knew least about in his own history finals exams, so that he could complete the answers in the time allotted. Hibbert, it was decided, was the most appropriate person to deal with the matter in hand; and he agreed to do so without a moment's fuss. 'I'm not a specialist in this field,' he said modestly, 'but I know a little about it, so if you will accept me as your supervisor, I am willing to supervise you.'

This offer was gratefully accepted by the stubborn young undergraduate standing in his study sipping a glass of sherry. So came about a strange state of affairs. The special subject about Muhammad, the rise of Islam and the early caliphate had not been offered before; and in that academic year, 1967-8, only this one, obdurate student took it; and the following year, owing to lack of interest, it was not offered again. For that single student, the course was his father's vision made real. It studied the life of the Prophet and the birth of the religion as events inside history, analytically, judiciously, *properly*. It might have been designed especially for him.

At the beginning of their work together Arthur Hibbert gave him a piece of advice he never forgot. 'You must never write history,' Hibbert said, 'until you can hear the people speak.' He thought about that for years, and in the end it came to feel like a valuable guiding principle for fiction as well. If you didn't have a sense of how people spoke, you didn't know them well enough, and so you couldn't – you *shouldn't* – tell their story. The way people spoke, in short, clipped phrases, or long, flowing rambles, revealed so much about them: their place of origin, their social class, their temperament, whether calm or angry, warm-hearted or cold-blooded, foul-mouthed or clean-spoken, polite or rude; and beneath their temperament, their true nature, intellectual or earthy, plain-spoken or devious, and, yes, good or bad. If that had been all he learned at Arthur's feet, it would have been enough. But he gained much more than that. He learned a world. And in that world one of the world's great religions was being born.

From the novel *Shame*

I KNOW SOMETHING of this immigrant business. I am an emigrant from one country (India) and a newcomer in two (England, where I live, and Pakistan, to which my family moved against my will). And I have a theory that the resentments we *mohajirs* engender have something to do with our conquest of the force of gravity. We have performed the act of which all men anciently dream, the thing for which they envy the birds; that is to say, we have flown.

I am comparing gravity with belonging. Both phenomena observably exist: my feet stay on the ground, and I have never been angrier than I was on the day my father told me he had sold my childhood home in Bombay. But neither is understood. We know the force of gravity, but not its origins; and to explain why we become attached to our birthplaces we pretend that we are trees and speak of roots. Look under your feet. You will not find gnarled growths sprouting through the soles. Roots, I sometimes think, are a conservative myth, designed to keep us in our places.

The anti-myths of gravity and of belonging bear the same name: flight. *Migration, n., moving, for instance in flight, from one place to another*. To fly and to flee: both are ways of seeking freedom ... an odd thing about gravity, incidentally, is that while it remains uncomprehended everybody seems to find it easy to comprehend the notion of its theoretical counter-force: anti-gravity. But anti-belonging is not accepted by modern science ... suppose ICI or Ciba-Geigy or Pfizer or Roche or even, I guess, NASA came up with an anti-gravity pill. The world's airlines would go broke overnight, of course. Pill-poppers would come unstuck from the ground and float upwards until they sank into the clouds. It would be necessary to devise special waterproof flying garments. And when the effects of the pill wore off one would simply sink gently down to earth again, but in a different place, because of prevailing windspeeds and planetary rotation. Personalized international travel could be made possible by manufacturing pills of different strengths for different lengths of journey. Some kind of directional booster-engine would have to be constructed, perhaps in back-pack form. Mass production could bring this within the reach of every household. You see the connection between gravity and 'roots': the pill would make migrants of us all. We would float upwards, use our boosters to get ourselves to the right latitude, and let the rotating planet do the rest.

When individuals come unstuck from their native land, they are called migrants. When nations do the same thing

(Bangladesh), the act is called secession. What is the best thing about migrant peoples and seceded nations? I think it is their hopefulness. Look into the eyes of such folk in old photographs. Hope blazes undimmed through the fading sepia tints. And what's the worst thing? It is the emptiness of one's luggage. I'm speaking of invisible suitcases, not the physical, perhaps cardboard, variety containing a few meaning-drained mementoes: we have come unstuck from more than land. We have floated upwards from history, from memory, from Time.

I may be such a person. Pakistan may be such a country.

It is well known that the term 'Pakistan', an acronym, was originally thought up in England by a group of Muslim intellectuals. P for the Punjabis, A for the Afghans, K for the Kashmiris, S for Sind and the 'tan', they say, for Baluchistan. (No mention of the East Wing, you notice; Bangladesh never got its name in the title, and so, eventually, it took the hint and seceded from the secessionists. Imagine what such a double secession does to people!) – So it was a word born in exile which then went East, was borne-across or trans-lated, and imposed itself on history; a returning migrant, settling down on partitioned land, forming a pal-impsest on the past. A palimpsest obscures what lies beneath. To build Pakistan it was necessary to cover up Indian history, to deny that Indian centuries lay just beneath the surface of Pakistani Standard Time. The past was rewritten; there was nothing else to be done.

Who commandeered the job of rewriting history? – The

immigrants, the *mohajirs*. In what languages? – Urdu and English, both imported tongues, although one travelled less distance than the other. It is possible to see the subsequent history of Pakistan as a duel between two layers of time, the obscured world forcing its way back through what-had-been-imposed. It is the true desire of every artist to impose his or her vision on the world; and Pakistan, the peeling, fragmenting palimpsest, increasingly at war with itself, may be described as a failure of the dreaming mind. Perhaps the pigments used were the wrong ones, impermanent, like Leonardo's; or perhaps the place was just *insufficiently imagined*, a picture full of irreconcilable elements, midriffbaring immigrant saris versus demure, indigenous Sindhi shalwar-kurtas, Urdu versus Punjabi, now versus then: a miracle that went wrong.

As for me: I, too, like all migrants, am a fantasist. I build imaginary countries and try to impose them on the ones that exist. I, too, face the problem of history: what to retain, what to dump, how to hold on to what memory insists on relinquishing, how to deal with change. And to come back to the 'roots' idea, I should say that I haven't managed to shake myself free of it completely. Sometimes I do see myself as a tree, even, rather grandly, as the ash Yggdrasil, the mythical world-tree of Norse legend. The ash Yggdrasil has three roots. One falls into the pool of knowledge by Valhalla, where Odin comes to drink. A second is being slowly consumed in the undying fire of Muspellheim, realm of the flame-god Surtur. The third is

I, like all migrants, am a fantasist. I build imaginary countries

gradually being gnawed through by a fearsome beast called the Nidhögg. And when fire and monster have destroyed two of the three, the ash will fall, and darkness will descend. The twilight of the gods: a tree's dream of death.

My story's palimpsest-country has, I repeat, no name of its own. The exiled Czech writer Kundera once wrote: 'A name means continuity with the past and people without a past are people without a name.' But I am dealing with a past that refuses to be suppressed, that is daily doing battle with the present; so it is perhaps unduly harsh of me to deny my fairyland a title.

There's an apocryphal story that Napier, after a successful campaign in what is now the south of Pakistan, sent back to England the guilty, one-word message, 'Peccavi'. *I have Sind*. I'm tempted to name my looking-glass Pakistan in honour of this bilingual (and fictional, because never really uttered) pun. Let it be *Peccavistan*.

An essay from *Imaginary Homelands*

AN OLD PHOTOGRAPH in a cheap frame hangs on a wall of the room where I work. It's a picture dating from 1946 of a house into which, at the time of its taking, I had not yet been born. The house is rather peculiar — a three storeyed gabled affair with tiled roofs and round towers in two corners, each wearing a pointy tiled hat. 'The past is a foreign country,' goes the famous opening sentence of L. P. Hartley's novel *The Go-Between*, 'they do things differently there.' But the photograph tells me to invert this idea; it reminds me that it's my present that is foreign, and that the past is home, albeit a lost home in a lost city in the mists of lost time.

A few years ago I revisited Bombay, which is my lost city, after an absence of something like half my life. Shortly after arriving, acting on an impulse, I opened the telephone directory and looked for my father's name. And, amazingly, there it was; his name, our old address, the unchanged telephone number, as if we had never gone away to the unmentionable country across the border. It was an eerie discovery. I felt as if I were being claimed, or informed that the facts of my faraway life were illusions, and that this continuity was the reality. Then I went to visit the house in the photograph and stood outside it, neither daring nor wishing to announce myself to its new owners. (I didn't want to see how they'd ruined the interior.) I was overwhelmed. The photograph had naturally been taken in black and white; and my memory, feeding on such images as this, had begun to see my childhood in the same way, monochromatically. The colours of my history had seeped out of my mind's eye; now my other two eyes were assaulted by colours, by the vividness of the red tiles, the yellow-edged green of cactus-leaves, the brilliance of bougainvillaea creeper. It is probably not too romantic to say that that was when my novel *Midnight's Children* was really born; when I realized how much I wanted to restore the past to myself, not in the faded greys of old family-album snapshots, but whole, in CinemaScope and glorious Technicolor.

Bombay is a city built by foreigners upon reclaimed land; I, who had been away so long that I almost qualified for the title, was gripped by the conviction that I, too, had a city and a history to reclaim.

It may be that writers in my position, exiles or emigrants or expatriates, are haunted by some sense of loss, some urge to reclaim, to look back, even at the risk of being mutated into pillars of salt. But if we do look back, we must also do so in the knowledge – which gives rise to profound uncertainties – that our physical alienation from India almost inevitably means that we will not be capable of reclaiming precisely the thing that was lost; that we will, in short, create fictions, not actual cities or villages, but invisible ones, imaginary homelands, Indias of the mind.

Writing my book in North London, looking out through my window on to a city scene totally unlike the ones I was imagining on to paper, I was constantly plagued by this problem, until I felt obliged to face it in the text, to make clear that (in spite of my original and I suppose somewhat Proustian ambition to unlock the gates of lost time so that the past reappeared as it actually had been, unaffected by the distortions of memory) what I was actually doing was a novel of memory and about memory, so that my India was just that: 'my' India, a version and no more than one version of all the hundreds of millions of possible versions. I tried to make it as imaginatively true as I could, but imaginative truth is simultaneously honourable and suspect, and I knew that my India may only have been one to which I (who am no longer what I was, and who by quitting Bombay never became what perhaps I was meant to be) was, let us say, willing to admit I belonged.

This is why I made my narrator, Saleem, suspect in his narration; his mistakes are the mistakes of a fallible memory compounded by quirks of character and of circumstance, and his vision is fragmentary. It may be that when the Indian writer who writes from outside India tries to reflect that world, he is obliged to deal in broken mirrors, some of whose fragments have been irretrievably lost.

BUT THERE IS a paradox here. The broken mirror may actually be as valuable as the one which is supposedly unflawed. Let me again try and explain this from my own experience. Before beginning *Midnight's Children*, I spent many months trying simply to recall as much of the Bombay of the 1950s and 1960s as I could; and not only Bombay – Kashmir, too, and Delhi and Aligarh, which, in my book, I've moved to Agra to heighten a certain joke about the Taj Mahal. I was genuinely amazed by how much came back to me. I found myself remembering what clothes people had worn on certain days, and school scenes, and whole passages of Bombay dialogue verbatim, or so it seemed; I even remembered advertisements, film-posters, the neon Jeep sign on Marine Drive, toothpaste ads for Binaca and for Kolynos, and a footbridge over the local railway line which bore, on one side, the legend 'Esso puts a tiger in your tank' and, on the other, the curiously contradictory admonition: 'Drive like Hell and you will get there.' Old songs came back to me from nowhere: a street entertainer's version of 'Good Night, Ladies', and, from the film *Mr 420* (a very appropriate source for my narrator to have used), the hit number

'Mera Joota Hai Japani',* which could almost be Saleem's theme song.

I knew that I had tapped a rich seam; but the point I want to make is that of course I'm not gifted with total recall, and it was precisely the partial nature of these memories, their fragmentation, that made them so evocative for me. The shards of memory acquired greater status, greater resonance, because they were *remains*; fragmentation made trivial things seem like symbols, and the mundane acquired numinous qualities. There is an obvious parallel here with archaeology. The broken pots of antiquity, from which the past can sometimes, but always provisionally, be reconstructed, are exciting to discover, even if they are pieces of the most quotidian objects.

It may be argued that the past is a country from which we have all emigrated, that its loss is part of our common

---

Mera joota hai Japani
Yé patloon Inglistani
Sar pé lal topi Rusi—
Phir bhi dil hai Hindustani
—which translates roughly as:
O, my shoes are Japanese
These trousers English, if you please
On my head, red Russian hat—
My heart's Indian for all that.
[This is also the song sung by Gibreel Farishta as he tumbles from the heavens at the beginning of *The Satanic Verses*.]

humanity. Which seems to me self-evidently true; but I suggest that the writer who is out-of-country and even out-of-language may experience this loss in an intensified form. It is made more concrete for him by the physical fact of discontinuity, of his present being in a different place from his past, of his being 'elsewhere'. This may enable him to speak properly and concretely on a subject of universal significance and appeal.

But let me go further. The broken glass is not merely a mirror of nostalgia. It is also, I believe, a useful tool with which to work in the present.

John Fowles begins *Daniel Martin* with the words: 'Whole sight: or all the rest is desolation.' But human beings do not perceive things whole; we are not gods but wounded creatures, cracked lenses, capable only of fractured perceptions. Partial beings, in all the senses of that phrase. Meaning is a shaky edifice we build out of scraps, dogmas, childhood injuries, newspaper articles, chance remarks, old films, small victories, people hated, people loved; perhaps it is because our sense of what is the case is constructed from such inadequate materials that we defend it so fiercely, even to the death. The Fowles position seems to me a way of succumbing to the guru-illusion. Writers are no longer sages, dispensing the wisdom of the centuries. And those of us who have been forced by cultural displacement to accept the provisional nature of all truths, all certainties, have perhaps had modernism forced upon us. We can't lay claim to Olympus, and are thus released to describe our worlds in the way in which all of us, whether writers or not, perceive it from day to day.

In *Midnight's Children*, my narrator Saleem uses, at one point, the metaphor of a cinema screen to discuss this business of perception: 'Suppose yourself in a large cinema, sitting at first in the back row, and gradually moving up, . . . until your nose is almost pressed against the screen. Gradually the stars' faces dissolve into dancing grain; tiny details assume grotesque proportions; . . . it becomes clear that the illusion itself is reality.' The movement towards the cinema screen is a metaphor for the narrative's movement through time towards the present, and the book itself, as it nears contemporary events, quite deliberately loses deep perspective, becomes more 'partial'. I wasn't trying to write about (for instance) the Emergency in the same way as I wrote about events half a century earlier. I felt it would be dishonest to pretend, when writing about the day before yesterday, that it was possible to see the whole picture. I showed certain blobs and slabs of the scene.

I ONCE TOOK part in a conference on modern writing at New College, Oxford. Various novelists, myself included, were talking earnestly of such matters as the need for new ways of describing the world. Then the playwright Howard Brenton suggested that this might be a somewhat limited aim: does literature seek to do no more than to describe? Flustered, all the novelists at once began talking about politics.

Let me apply Brenton's question to the specific case of Indian writers, in England, writing about India. Can they do no more than describe, from a distance, the world that they have left? Or does the distance open any other doors?

These are of course political questions, and must be answered at least partly in political terms. I must say first of all that description is itself a political act. The black American writer Richard Wright once wrote that black and white Americans were engaged in a war over the nature of reality. Their descriptions were incompatible. So it is clear that redescribing a world is the necessary first step towards changing it. And particularly at times when the State takes reality into its own hands, and sets about distorting it, altering the past to fit its present needs, then the making of the alternative realities of art, including the novel of memory, becomes politicized. 'The struggle of man against power,' Milan Kundera has written, 'is the struggle of memory against forgetting.' Writers and politicians are natural rivals. Both groups try to make the world in their own images; they fight for the same territory. And the novel is one way of denying the official, politicians' version of truth.

The 'State truth' about the war in Bangladesh, for instance, is that no atrocities were committed by the Pakistani army in what was then the East Wing. This version is sanctified by many persons who would describe themselves as intellectuals. And the official version of the Emergency in India was well expressed by Mrs Gandhi in a recent BBC interview. She said that there were some people around who claimed that bad things had happened during the Emergency, forced sterilizations, things like that; but, she stated, this was all false. Nothing of this type had ever occurred. The interviewer, Mr Robert Kee, did not probe this statement at all. Instead he told Mrs Gandhi and the *Panorama* audience that she had proved, many times over, her right to be called a democrat.

So literature can, and perhaps must, give the lie to official facts. But is this a proper function of those of us who write from outside India? Or are we just dilettantes in such affairs, because we are not involved in their day-to-day unfolding, because by speaking out we take no risks, because our personal safety is not threatened? What right do we have to speak at all?

My answer is very simple. Literature is self-validating. That is to say, a book is not justified by its author's worthiness to write it, but by the quality of what has been written. There are terrible books that arise directly out of experience, and extraordinary imaginative feats dealing with themes which the author has been obliged to approach from the outside.

Literature is not in the business of copyrighting certain themes for certain groups. And as for risk: the real risks of any artist are taken in the work, in pushing the work to the limits of what is possible, in the attempt to increase the sum of what it is possible to think. Books become good when they go to this edge and risk falling over it – when they endanger the artist by reason of what he has, or has not, *artistically* dared.

So if I am to speak for Indian writers in England I would say this, paraphrasing G. V. Desani's H. Hatterr: The migrations of the fifties and sixties happened. 'We are. We are here.' And we are not willing to be excluded from any part of our heritage; which heritage includes both a Bradford-born Indian kid's right to be treated as a full member of British society, and also the right of any member of this post-diaspora community to draw on its roots for its art, just as all the world's community of displaced writers has always done. (I'm thinking, for instance, of Grass's Danzig-become-Gdansk, of Joyce's abandoned Dublin, of Isaac Bashevis Singer and Maxine Hong Kingston and Milan Kundera and many others. It's a long list.)

Let me override at once the faintly defensive note that has crept into these last few remarks. The Indian writer, looking back at India, does so through guilt-tinted spectacles. (I am of course, once more, talking about myself.) I am speaking now of those of us who emigrated . . . and I suspect that there are times when the move seems wrong to us all, when we seem, to ourselves, post-lapsarian men and women. We are Hindus who have crossed the black water; we are Muslims who eat pork. And as a result – as my use of the Christian notion of the Fall indicates – we are now partly of the West. Our identity is at once plural and partial. Sometimes we feel that we straddle two cultures; at other times, that we fall between two stools. But however ambiguous and shifting this ground may be, it is not an infertile territory for a writer to occupy. If literature is in part the business of finding new angles at which to enter reality, then once again our distance, our long geographical perspective, may provide us with such angles. Or it may be that that is simply what we must think in order to do our work.

Midnight's Children enters its subject from the point of view of a secular man. I am a member of that generation of Indians who were sold the secular ideal. One of the things I liked, and still like, about India is that it is based on a non-sectarian philosophy. I was not raised in a narrowly Muslim environment; I do not consider Hindu culture to be either alien from me or more important than the Islamic heritage. I believe this has something to do with the nature of Bombay, a metropolis in which the multiplicity of commingled faiths and cultures curiously creates a remarkably secular ambience. Saleem Sinai makes use, eclectically, of whatever elements from whatever sources he chooses. It may have been easier for his author to do this from outside modern India than inside it.

I want to make one last point about the description of India that *Midnight's Children* attempts. It is a point about pessimism. The book has been criticised in India for its allegedly despairing tone. And the despair of the writer-from-outside may indeed look a little easy, a little pat. But I do not see the book as despairing or nihilistic. The point of view of the narrator is not entirely that of the author.

What I tried to do was to set up a tension in the text, a paradoxical opposition between the form and content of the narrative. The story of Saleem does indeed lead him to despair. But the story is told in a manner designed to echo, as closely as my abilities allowed, the Indian talent for non-stop self-regeneration. This is why the narrative constantly throws up new stories, why it 'teems'. The form – multitudinous, hinting at the infinite possibilities of the country – is the optimistic counterweight to Saleem's personal tragedy. I do not think that a book written in such a manner can really be called a despairing work.

ENGLAND'S INDIAN WRITERS are by no means all the same type of animal. Some of us, for instance, are Pakistani. Others Bangladeshi. Others West, or East, or even South African. And V. S. Naipaul, by now, is something else entirely. This word 'Indian' is getting to be a pretty scattered concept. Indian writers in England include political exiles, first-generation migrants, affluent expatriates whose residence here is frequently temporary, naturalized Britons, and people born here who may never have laid eyes on the subcontinent. Clearly, nothing that I say can apply across all these categories. But one of the interesting things about this diverse community is that, as far as Indo-British fiction is concerned, its existence changes the ball game, because that fiction is in future going to come as much from addresses in London, Birmingham and Yorkshire as from Delhi or Bombay.

One of the changes has to do with attitudes towards the use of English. Many have referred to the argument about the appropriateness of this language to Indian themes. And I hope all of us share the view that we can't simply use the language in the way the British did; that it needs remaking for our own purposes. Those of us who do use English do so in spite of our ambiguity towards it, or perhaps because of that, perhaps because we can find in that linguistic struggle a reflection of other struggles taking place in the real world, struggles between the cultures within ourselves and the influences at work upon our societies. To conquer English may be to complete the process of making ourselves free.

But the British Indian writer simply does not have the option of rejecting English, anyway. His children, her children, will grow up speaking it, probably as a first language; and in the forging of a British Indian identity the English language is of central importance. It must, in spite of everything, be embraced. (The word 'translation' comes, etymologically, from the Latin for 'bearing across'. Having been borne across the world, we are translated men. It is normally supposed that something always gets lost in translation; I cling, obstinately, to the notion that something can also be gained.)

To be an Indian writer in this society is to face, every day, problems of definition. What does it mean to be 'Indian' outside India? How can culture be preserved without becoming ossified? How should we discuss the need for change within ourselves and our community without seeming to play into the hands of our racial enemies? What are the consequences, both spiritual and practical, of refusing to make any concessions to Western ideas and practices? What are the consequences of embracing those ideas and practices and turning away from the ones that came here with us? These questions are all a single, existential question: How are we to live in the world?

I do not propose to offer, prescriptively, any answers to these questions; only to state that these are some of the issues with which each of us will have to come to terms.

To TURN MY eyes outwards now, and to say a little about the relationship between the Indian writer and the majority white culture in whose midst he lives, and with which his work will sooner or later have to deal:

In common with many Bombay-raised middle-class children of my generation, I grew up with an intimate knowledge of, and even sense of friendship with, a certain kind of England: a dream-England composed of Test Matches at Lord's presided over by the voice of John Arlott, at which Freddie Trueman bowled unceasingly and without success at Polly Umrigar; of Enid Blyton and Billy Bunter, in which we were even prepared to smile indulgently at portraits such as 'Hurree Jamset Ram Singh', 'the dusky nabob of Bhanipur'. I wanted to come to England. I couldn't wait. And to be fair, England has done all right by me; but I find it a little difficult to be properly grateful. I can't escape the view that my relatively easy ride is not the result of the dream-England's famous sense of tolerance and fair play, but of my social class, my freak fair skin and my 'English' English accent. Take away any of these, and the story would have been very different. Because of course the dream-England is no more than a dream.

Sadly, it's a dream from which too many white Britons refuse to awake. Recently, on a live radio programme, a professional humorist asked me, in all seriousness, why I objected to being called a wog. He said he had always thought it a rather charming word, a term of endearment. 'I was at the zoo the other day,' he revealed, 'and a zoo keeper told me that the wogs were best with the animals; they stuck their fingers in their ears and wiggled them about and the animals felt at home.' The ghost of Hurree Jamset Ram Singh walks among us still.

As Richard Wright found long ago in America, black and white descriptions of society are no longer compatible. Fantasy, or the mingling of fantasy and naturalism, is one way of dealing with these problems. It offers a way of echoing in the form of our work the issues faced by all of us: how to build a new, 'modern' world out of an old, legend-haunted civilization, an old culture which we have brought into the heart of a newer one. But whatever technical solutions we may find, Indian writers in these islands, like others who have migrated into the north from the south, are capable of writing from a kind of double perspective: because they, we, are at one and the same time insiders and outsiders in this society. This stereoscopic vision is perhaps what we can offer in place of 'whole sight'.

THERE IS ONE last idea that I should like to explore, even though it may, on first hearing, seem to contradict much of what I've so far said. It is this: of all the many elephant traps lying ahead of us, the largest and most dangerous pitfall would be the adoption of a ghetto mentality. To forget that there is a world beyond the community to which we belong, to confine ourselves within narrowly defined cultural frontiers, would be, I believe, to go voluntarily into that form of internal exile which in South Africa is called the 'homeland'. We must guard against creating, for the most virtuous of reasons, British–Indian literary equivalents of Bophuthatswana or the Transkei.

This raises immediately the question of whom one is writing 'for'. My own, short, answer is that I have never had a reader in mind. I have ideas, people, events, shapes, and I write 'for' those things, and hope that the completed work will be of interest to others. But which others? In the case of *Midnight's Children* I certainly felt that if its subcontinental readers had rejected the work, I should have thought it a failure, no matter what the reaction in the West. So I would say that I write 'for' people who feel part of the things I write 'about', but also for everyone else whom I can reach. In this I am of the same opinion as the black American writer Ralph Ellison, who, in his collection

The largest and most dangerous pitfall would be the adoption of a ghetto mentality

of essays *Shadow and Act*, says that he finds something precious in being black in America at this time; but that he is also reaching for more than that. 'I was taken very early,' he writes, 'with a passion to link together all I loved within the Negro community and all those things I felt in the world which lay beyond.'

Art is a passion of the mind. And the imagination works best when it is most free. Western writers have always felt free to be eclectic in their selection of theme, setting, form; Western visual artists have, in this century, been happily raiding the visual storehouses of Africa, Asia, the Philippines. I am sure that we must grant ourselves an equal freedom.

Let me suggest that Indian writers in England have access to a second tradition, quite apart from their own racial history. It is the culture and political history of the phenomenon of migration, displacement, life in a minority group. We can quite legitimately claim as our ancestors the Huguenots, the Irish, the Jews; the past to which we belong is an English past, the history of immigrant Britain. Swift, Conrad, Marx are as much our literary forebears as Tagore or Ram Mohan Roy. America, a nation of immigrants, has created great literature out of the phenomenon of cultural transplantation, out of examining the ways in which people cope with a new world; it may be that by discovering what we have in common with those who preceded us into this country, we can begin to do the same.

I stress this is only one of many possible strategies. But

we are inescapably international writers at a time when the novel has never been a more international form (a writer like Borges speaks of the influence of Robert Louis Stevenson on his work; Heinrich Boll acknowledges the influence of Irish literature; cross-pollination is everywhere); and it is perhaps one of the more pleasant freedoms of the literary migrant to be able to choose his parents. My own – selected half consciously, half not – include Gogol, Cervantes, Kafka, Melville, Machado de Assis; a polyglot family tree, against which I measure myself, and to which I would be honoured to belong.

There's a beautiful image in Saul Bellow's latest novel, *The Dean's December*. The central character, the Dean, Corde, hears a dog barking wildly somewhere. He imagines that the barking is the dog's protest against the limit of dog experience. 'For God's sake,' the dog is saying, 'open the universe a little more!' And because Bellow is, of course, not really talking about dogs, or not only about dogs, I have the feeling that the dog's rage, and its desire, is also mine, ours, everyone's. 'For God's sake, open the universe a little more!'

The Courter
A story from *East, West*

1

CERTAINLY-MARY WAS THE smallest woman Mixed-Up the hall porter had come across, dwarfs excepted, a tiny sixty-year-old Indian lady with her greying hair tied behind her head in a neat bun, hitching up her red-hemmed white sari in the front and negotiating the apartment block's front steps as if they were Alps. 'No,' he said aloud, furrowing his brow. What would be the right peaks. Ah, good, that was the name. 'Ghats,' he said proudly. Word from a schoolboy atlas long ago, when India felt as far away as Paradise. (Nowadays Paradise seemed even further away but India, and Hell, had come a good bit closer.) 'Western Ghats, Eastern Ghats, and now Kensington Ghats,' he said, giggling. 'Mountains.'

She stopped in front of him in the oak-panelled lobby. 'But ghats in India are also stairs,' she said. 'Yes yes certainly. For instance in Hindu holy city of Varanasi, where the Brahmins sit taking the filgrims' money is called Dasashwamedh-ghat. Broad-broad staircase down to River Ganga. O, most certainly! Also Manikarnika-ghat. They buy fire from a house with a tiger leaping from the roof – yes certainly, a statue tiger, coloured by Technicolor, what are you thinking? – and they bring it in a box to set fire to their loved ones' bodies. Funeral fires are of sandal. Photographs not allowed; no, certainly not.'

HE BEGAN THINKING of her as Certainly-Mary because she never said plain yes or no; always this O-yes-certainly or no-certainly-not. In the confused circumstances that had prevailed ever since his brain, his one sure thing, had let him down, he could hardly be certain of anything any more; so he was stunned by her sureness, first into nostalgia, then envy, then attraction. And attraction was a thing so long forgotten that when the churning started he thought for a long time it must be the Chinese dumplings he had brought home from the High Street carry-out.

ENGLISH WAS HARD for Certainly-Mary, and this was a part of what drew damaged old Mixed-Up towards her. The letter p was a particular problem, often turning into an f or a c; when she proceeded through the lobby with a wheeled wicker shopping basket, she would say, 'Going shocking,' and when, on her return, he offered to help lift the basket up the front ghats, she would answer, 'Yes, fleas.' As the elevator lifted her away, she called through the grille: 'Oé, courter! Thank you, courter. O, yes, certainly.' (In Hindi and Konkani, however, her p's knew their place.)

So: thanks to her unexpected, somehow stomach-churning magic, he was no longer porter but courter. 'Courter,' he repeated to the mirror when she had gone. His breath made a little dwindling picture of the word on the glass. 'Courter courter caught.' Okay. People called him many things, he did not mind. But this name, this courter, this he would try to be.

2

FOR YEARS NOW I've been meaning to write down the story of Certainly-Mary, our ayah, the woman who did as much as my mother to raise my sisters and me, and her great adventure with her 'courter' in London, where we all lived for a time in the early Sixties in a block called Waverley House; but what with one thing and another I never got round to it.

Then recently I heard from Certainly-Mary after a longish silence. She wrote to say that she was ninety-one, had had a serious operation, and would I kindly send her some money, because she was embarrassed that her niece, with whom she was now living in the Kurla district of Bombay, was so badly out of pocket.

I sent the money, and soon afterwards received a pleasant letter from the niece, Stella, written in the same hand as the letter from 'Aya' – as we had always called Mary, palindromically dropping the 'h'. Aya had been so touched, the niece wrote, that I remembered her after all these years. 'I have been hearing the stories about you folks all my life,' the letter went on, 'and I think of you a little bit as family. Maybe you recall my mother Mary's sister. She unfortunately passed on. Now it is I who write Mary's letters for her. We all wish you the best.'

This message from an intimate stranger reached out to me in my enforced exile from the beloved country of my birth and moved me, stirring things that had been buried very deep. Of course it also made me feel guilty about having done so little for Mary over the years. For whatever reason, it has become more important than ever to set down the story I've been carrying around unwritten for so long, the story of Aya and the gentle man whom she renamed – with unintentional but prophetic overtones of romance – 'the courter'. I see now that it is not just their story, but ours, mine, as well.

3

HIS REAL NAME was Mecir: you were supposed to say Mishirsh because it had invisible accents on it in some Iron Curtain language in which the accents had to be invisible, my sister Durré said solemnly, in case somebody spied on them or rubbed them out or something. His first name also began with an m but it was so full of what we called Communist consonants, all those z's and c's and w's walled up together without vowels to give them breathing space, that I never even tried to learn it.

At first we thought of nicknaming him after a mischievous little comic-book character, Mr Mxyztplk from the Fifth Dimension, who looked a bit like Elmer Fudd and used to make Superman's life hell until ole Supe could trick him into saying his name backwards, Klptzyxm, whereupon he disappeared back into the Fifth Dimension; but because we weren't too sure how to say Mxyztplk (not to mention Klptzyxm) we dropped that idea. 'We'll just call you Mixed-Up,' I told him in the end, to simplify life. 'Mishter Mikshed-Up Mishirsh.' I was fifteen then and bursting with unemployed cock and it meant I could say things like that right into people's faces, even people less accommodating than Mr Mecir with his stroke.

WHAT I REMEMBER most vividly are his pink rubber washing-up gloves, which he seemed never to remove, at least not until he came calling for Certainly-Mary . . . At any rate, when I insulted him, with my sisters Durré and Muneeza cackling in the lift, Mecir just grinned an empty good-natured grin, nodded, 'You call me what you like, okay,' and went back to buffing and polishing the brasswork. There was no point teasing him if he was going to be like that, so I got into the lift and all the way to the fourth floor we sang *I Can't Stop Loving You* at the top of our best Ray Charles voices, which were pretty awful. But we were wearing our dark glasses, so it didn't matter.

4

IT WAS THE summer of 1962, and school was out. My baby sister Scheherazade was just one year old. Durré was a bee-hived fourteen; Muneeza was ten, and already quite a handful. The three of us – or rather Durré and me, with Muneeza trying desperately and unsuccessfully to be included in our gang – would stand over Scheherazade's cot and sing to her. 'No nursery rhymes,' Durré had decreed, and so there were none, for though she was a year my junior she was a natural leader. The infant Scheherazade's lullabies were our cover versions of recent hits by Chubby Checker, Neil Sedaka, Elvis and Pat Boone.

'Why don't you come home, Speedy Gonzales?' we bellowed in sweet disharmony: but most of all, and with actions, we would jump down, turn around and pick a bale of cotton. We would have jumped down, turned around and picked those bales all day except that the Maharaja of B— in the flat below complained, and Aya Mary came in to plead with us to be quiet.

'Look, see, it's Jumble-Aya who's fallen for Mixed-Up,' Durré shouted, and Mary blushed a truly immense blush. So naturally we segued right into a quick me-oh-my-oh; son of a gun, we had big fun. But then the baby began to yell, my father came in with his head down bull-fashion and steaming from both ears, and we needed all the good luck charms we could find.

I HAD BEEN at boarding school in England for a year or so when Abba took the decision to bring the family over. Like all his decisions, it was neither explained to nor discussed with anyone, not even my mother. When they first arrived he rented two adjacent flats in a seedy Bayswater mansion block called Graham Court, which lurked furtively in a nothing street that crawled along the side of the ABC Queensway cinema towards the Porchester Baths. He commandeered one of these flats for himself and put my mother, three sisters and Aya in the other; also, on school holidays, me. England, where liquor was freely available, did little for my father's *bonhomie*, so in a way it was a relief to have a flat to ourselves.

Most nights he emptied a bottle of Johnnie Walker Red Label and a soda-siphon. My mother did not dare to go across to 'his place' in the evenings. She said: 'He makes faces at me.'

Aya Mary took Abba his dinner and answered all his calls (if he wanted anything, he would phone us up and ask for it). I am not sure why Mary was spared his drunken rages. She said it was because she was nine years his senior so she could tell him to show due respect.

AFTER A FEW months, however, my father leased a three-bedroom fourth-floor apartment with a fancy address. This was Waverley House in Kensington Court, W8. Among its other residents were not one but two Indian Maharajas, the sporting Prince P— as well as the old B— who has already been mentioned. Now we were jammed in together, my parents and Baby Scare-zade (as her siblings had affectionately begun to call her) in the master bedroom, the three of us in a much smaller room, and Mary, I regret to admit, on a straw mat laid on the fitted carpet in the hall. The third bedroom became my father's office, where he made phone-calls and kept his *Encyclopaedia Britannica*, his *Reader's Digests*, and (under lock and key) the television cabinet. We entered it at our peril. It was the Minotaur's lair.

ONE MORNING HE was persuaded to drop in at the corner pharmacy and pick up some supplies for the baby. When he returned there was a hurt, schoolboyish look on his face that I had never seen before, and he was pressing his hand against his cheek.

'She hit me,' he said plaintively.

'Hai! Allah-tobah! Darling!' cried my mother, fussing. 'Who hit you? Are you injured? Show me, let me see.'

'I did nothing,' he said, standing there in the hall with the pharmacy bag in his other hand and a face as pink as Mecir's rubber gloves. 'I just went in with your list. The girl seemed very helpful. I asked for baby compound, Johnson's powder, teething jelly, and she brought them out. Then I asked did she have any nipples, and she slapped my face.'

My mother was appalled. 'Just for that?' And Certainly-Mary backed her up. 'What is this nonsense?' she wanted to know. 'I have been in that chemist's shock, and they have flenty nickels, different sizes, all on view.'

Durré and Muneeza could not contain themselves. They were rolling round on the floor, laughing and kicking their legs in the air.

'You both shut your face at once,' my mother ordered. 'A madwoman has hit your father. Where is the comedy?'

'I don't believe it,' Durré gasped. 'You just went up to that girl and said,' and here she fell apart again, stamping her feet and holding her stomach, '"*have you got any nipples?*"'

My father grew thunderous, empurpled. Durré controlled herself. 'But Abba,' she said, at length, 'here they call them teats.'

Now my mother's and Mary's hands flew to their mouths, and even my father looked shocked. 'But how shameless!' my mother said. 'The same word as for what's on your bosoms?' She coloured, and stuck out her tongue for shame.

'These English,' sighed Certainly-Mary. 'But aren't they the limit? Certainly-yes; they are.'

I REMEMBER THIS story with delight, because it was the only time I ever saw my father so discomfited, and the incident became legendary and the girl in the pharmacy was installed as the object of our great veneration. (Durré and

I went in there just to take a look at her – she was a plain, short girl of about seventeen, with large, unavoidable breasts – but she caught us whispering and glared so fiercely that we fled.) And also because in the general hilarity I was able to conceal the shaming truth that I, who had been in England for so long, would have made the same mistake as Abba did.

It wasn't just Certainly-Mary and my parents who had trouble with the English language. My schoolfellows tittered when in my Bombay way I said 'brought-up' for upbringing (as in 'where was your brought-up?') and 'thrice' for three times and 'quarter-plate' for side-plate and 'macaroni' for pasta in general. As for learning the difference between nipples and teats, I really hadn't had any opportunities to increase my word power in that area at all.

5

So I was a little jealous of Certainly-Mary when Mixed-Up came to call. He rang our bell, his body quivering with deference in an old suit grown too loose, the trousers tightly gathered by a belt; he had taken off his rubber gloves and there were roses in his hand. My father opened the door and gave him a withering look. Being a snob, Abba was not pleased that the flat lacked a separate service entrance, so that even a porter had to be treated as a member of the same universe as himself.

'Mary,' Mixed-Up managed, licking his lips and pushing back his floppy white hair. 'I, to see Miss Mary, come, am.'

'Wait on,' Abba said, and shut the door in his face.

CERTAINLY-MARY SPENT ALL her afternoons off with old Mixed-Up from then on, even though that first date was not a complete success. He took her 'up West' to show her the visitors' London she had never seen, but at the top of an up escalator at Piccadilly Circus, while Mecir was painfully enunciating the words on the posters she couldn't read – *Unzip a banana*, and *Idris when I's dri* – she got her sari stuck in the jaws of the machine, and as the escalator pulled at the garment it began to unwind. She was forced to spin round and round like a top, and screamed at the top of her voice, 'O BAAP! BAAPU-RÉ! BAAP-RÉ-BAAP-RÉ-BAAP!' It was Mixed-Up who saved her by pushing the emergency stop button before the sari was completely unwound and she was exposed in her petticoat for all the world to see.

'O, courter!' she wept on his shoulder. 'O, no more escaleater, courter, nevermore, surely not!'

MY OWN AMOROUS longings were aimed at Durré's best friend, a Polish girl called Rozalia, who had a holiday job at Faiman's shoe shop on Oxford Street. I pursued her pathetically throughout the holidays and, on and off, for the next two years. She would let me have lunch with her sometimes and buy her a Coke and a sandwich, and once she came with me to stand on the terraces at White Hart Lane to watch Jimmy Greaves's first game for the Spurs. 'Come on you whoi-oites,' we both shouted dutifully. 'Come on you *Lily-whoites*.' After that she even invited me into the back room at Faiman's, where she kissed me twice and let me touch her breast, but that was as far as I got.

AND THEN THERE was my sort-of-cousin Chandni, whose mother's sister had married my mother's brother though they had since split up. Chandni was eighteen months older than me, and so sexy it made you sick. She was training to be an Indian classical dancer, Odissi as well as Natyam, but in the meantime she dressed in tight black jeans and a clinging black polo-neck jumper and took me, now and then, to hang out at Bunjie's, where she knew most of the folk-music crowd that frequented the place, and where she answered to the name of Moonlight, which is what *chandni* means. I chain-smoked with the folkies and then went to the toilet to throw up.

Chandni was the stuff of obsessions. She was a teenage dream, the Moon River come to Earth like the Goddess Ganga, dolled up in slinky black. But for her I was just the young greenhorn cousin to whom she was being nice because he hadn't learned his way around.

SHE-E-RRY, WON'T YOU *come out tonight?* yodelled the Four Seasons. I knew exactly how they felt. *Come, come, come out toni-yi-yight.* And while you're at it, love me do.

6

THEY WENT FOR walks in Kensington Gardens. 'Pan,' Mixed-Up said, pointing at a statue. 'Los' boy. Nev' grew up.' They went to Barkers and Pontings and Derry & Toms and picked out furniture and curtains for imaginary homes. They cruised supermarkets and chose little delicacies to eat. In Mecir's cramped lounge they sipped what he called 'chimpanzee tea' and toasted crumpets in front of an electric bar fire.

THANKS TO MIXED-UP, Mary was at last able to watch television. She liked children's programmes best, especially *The Flintstones*. Once, giggling at her daring, Mary confided to Mixed-Up that Fred and Wilma reminded her of her Sahib and Begum Sahiba upstairs; at which the courter, matching her audaciousness, pointed first at Certainly-Mary and then at himself, grinned a wide gappy smile and said, 'Rubble.'

Later, on the news, a vulpine Englishman with a thin moustache and mad eyes declaimed a warning about immigrants, and Certainly-Mary flapped her hand at the set: 'Khali-pili bom marta,' she objected, and then, for her host's benefit translated: 'For nothing he is shouting shouting. Bad life! Switch it off.'

THEY WERE OFTEN interrupted by the Maharajas of B— and P—, who came downstairs to escape their wives and ring other women from the call-box in the porter's room.

'Oh, baby, forget that guy,' said sporty Prince P—, who seemed to spend all his days in tennis whites, and whose plump gold Rolex was almost lost in the thick hair on his arm. 'I'll show you a better time than him, baby; step into my world.'

The Maharaja of B— was older, uglier; more matter-of-fact. 'Yes, bring all appliances. Room is booked in name of Mr Douglas Home. Six forty-five to seven fifteen. You have printed rate card? Please. Also a two-foot ruler, must be wooden. Frilly apron, plus.'

THIS IS WHAT has lasted in my memory of Waverley House, this seething mass of bad marriages, booze, philanderers and unfulfilled young lusts; of the Maharaja of P— roaring away towards London's casinoland every night, in a red sports car with fitted blondes, and of the Maharaja of B— skulking off to Kensington High Street wearing dark glasses in the dark, and a coat with the collar turned up even though it was high summer; and at the heart of our little universe were Certainly-Mary and her courter, drinking chimpanzee tea and singing along with the national anthem of Bedrock.

But they were not really like Barney and Betty Rubble at all. They were formal, polite. They were . . . courtly. He courted her, and, like a coy, ringleted ingénue with a fan, she inclined her head, and entertained his suit.

7

I SPENT ONE half-term weekend in 1963 at the home in Beccles, Suffolk of Field Marshal Sir Charles Lutwidge-Dodgson, an old India hand and a family friend who was supporting my application for British citizenship. 'The Dodo', as he was known, invited me down by myself, saying he wanted to get to know me better.

He was a huge man whose skin had started hanging too loosely on his face, a giant living in a tiny thatched cottage and forever bumping his head. No wonder he was irascible at times; he was in Hell, a Gulliver trapped in that rose-garden Lilliput of croquet hoops, church bells, sepia photographs and old battle-trumpets.

The weekend was fitful and awkward until the Dodo asked if I played chess. Slightly awestruck at the prospect of playing a Field Marshal, I nodded; and ninety minutes later, to my amazement, won the game.

I went into the kitchen, strutting somewhat, planning to boast a little to the old soldier's long-time housekeeper, Mrs Liddell. But as soon as I entered she said: 'Don't tell me. You never went and won?'

'Yes,' I said, affecting nonchalance. 'As a matter of fact, yes, I did.'

'Gawd,' said Mrs Liddell. 'Now there'll be hell to pay. You go back in there and ask him for another game, and this time make sure you lose.'

I did as I was told, but was never invited to Beccles again.

STILL, THE DEFEAT of the Dodo gave me new confidence at the chessboard, so when I returned to Waverley House after finishing my O levels, and was at once invited to play a game by Mixed-Up (Mary had told him about my victory in the Battle of Beccles with great pride and some hyperbole), I said: 'Sure, I don't mind.' How long could it take to thrash the old duffer, after all?

There followed a massacre royal. Mixed-Up did not just beat me; he had me for breakfast, over easy. I couldn't believe it – the canny opening, the fluency of his combination play, the force of his attacks, my own impossibly cramped, strangled positions – and asked for a second game. This time he tucked into me even more heartily. I sat broken in my chair at the end, close to tears. *Big girls don't cry*, I reminded myself, but the song went on playing in my head: *That's just an alibi*.

'Who are you?' I demanded, humiliation weighing down every syllable. 'The devil in disguise?'

Mixed-Up gave his big, silly grin. 'Grand Master,' he said. 'Long time. Before head.'

'YOU'RE A GRAND Master,' I repeated, still in a daze. Then in a moment of horror I remembered that I had seen the name Mecir in books of classic games. 'Nimzo-Indian,' I said aloud. He beamed and nodded furiously.

'That Mecir?' I asked wonderingly.

'That,' he said. There was saliva dribbling out of a corner of his sloppy old mouth. This ruined old man was in the books. He was in the books. And even with his mind turned to rubble he could still wipe the floor with me.

'Now play lady,' he grinned. I didn't get it. 'Mary lady,' he said. 'Yes yes certainly.'

She was pouring tea, waiting for my answer. 'Aya, you can't play,' I said, bewildered.

'Learning, baba,' she said. 'What is it, na? Only a game.'

And then she, too, beat me senseless, and with the black pieces, at that. It was not the greatest day of my life.

8

FROM 100 MOST *Instructive Chess Games* by Robert Reshevsky, 1961:

> *M. Mecir – M. Najdorf*
> *Dallas 1950, Nimzo-Indian Defense*
> The attack of a tactician can be troublesome to meet – that of a strategist even more so. Whereas the tactician's threats may be unmistakable, the strategist confuses the issue by keeping things in abeyance. He threatens to threaten!
>
> Take this game for instance: Mecir posts a Knight at Q6 to get a grip on the center. Then he establishes a passed Pawn on one wing to occupy his opponent on

the Queen side. Finally he stirs up the position on the King-side. What does the poor bewildered opponent do? How can he defend everything at once? Where will the blow fall?

Watch Mecir keep Najdorf on the run, as he shifts the attack from side to side!

Chess had become their private language. Old Mixed-Up, lost as he was for words, retained, on the chessboard, much of the articulacy and subtlety which had vanished from his speech. As Certainly-Mary gained in skill – and she had learned with astonishing speed, I thought bitterly, for someone who couldn't read or write or pronounce the letter p – she was better able to understand, and respond to, the wit of the reduced maestro with whom she had so unexpectedly forged a bond.

He taught her with great patience, showing-not-telling, repeating openings and combinations and endgame techniques over and over until she began to see the meaning in the patterns. When they played, he handicapped himself, he told her her best moves and demonstrated their consequences, drawing her, step by step, into the infinite possibilities of the game.

SUCH WAS THEIR courtship. 'It is like an adventure, baba,' Mary once tried to explain to me. 'It is like going with him to his country, you know? What a place, baap-ré! Beautiful and dangerous and funny and full of fuzzles. For me it is a big-big discovery. What to tell you? I go for the game. It is a wonder.'

I understood, then, how far things had gone between them. Certainly-Mary had never married, and had made it clear to old Mixed-Up that it was too late to start any of that monkey business at her age. The courter was a widower, and had grown-up children somewhere, lost long ago behind the ever-higher walls of Eastern Europe. But in the game of chess they had found a form of flirtation, an endless renewal that precluded the possibility of boredom, a courtly wonderland of the ageing heart.

What would the Dodo have made of it all? No doubt it would have scandalised him to see chess, chess of all games, the great formalisation of war, transformed into an art of love.

As for me: my defeats by Certainly-Mary and her courter ushered in further humiliations. Durré and Muneeza went down with the mumps, and so, finally, in spite of my mother's efforts to segregate us, did I. I lay terrified in bed while the doctor warned me not to stand up and move around if I could possibly help it. 'If you do,' he said, 'your parents won't need to punish you. You will have punished yourself quite enough.'

I spent the following few weeks tormented day and night by visions of grotesquely swollen testicles and a subsequent life of limp impotence – finished before I'd even started, it wasn't fair! – which were made much worse by my sisters' quick recovery and incessant gibes. But in the end I was lucky; the illness didn't spread to the deep South. 'Think how happy your hundred and one girlfriends will be, bhai,' sneered Durré, who knew all about my continued failures in the Rozalia and Chandni departments.

On the radio, people were always singing about the joys of being sixteen years old. I wondered where they were, all those boys and girls of my age having the time of their lives. Were they driving around America in Studebaker convertibles? They certainly weren't in my neighbourhood. London, W8 was Sam Cooke country that summer. *Another Saturday night* ... There might be a mop-top love-song stuck at number one, but I was down with lonely Sam in the lower depths of the charts, how-I-wishing I had someone, etc., and generally feeling in a pretty goddamn dreadful way.

9

'BABA, COME QUICK.'

It was late at night when Aya Mary shook me awake. After many urgent hisses, she managed to drag me out of sleep and pull me, pajama'ed and yawning, down the hall. On the landing outside our flat was Mixed-Up the courter, huddled up against a wall, weeping. He had a black eye and there was dried blood on his mouth.

'What happened?' I asked Mary, shocked.

'Men,' wailed Mixed-Up. 'Threaten. Beat.'

He had been in his lounge earlier that evening when the

sporting Maharaja of P— burst in to say, 'If anybody comes looking for me, okay, any tough-guy type guys, okay, I am out, okay? Oh you tea. Don't let them go upstairs, okay? Big tip, okay?'

A short time later, the old Maharaja of B— also arrived in Mecir's lounge, looking distressed.

'Suno, listen on,' said the Maharaja of B—. 'You don't know where I am, samajh liya? Understood? Some low persons may inquire. You don't know. I am abroad, achha? On extended travels abroad. Do your job, porter. Handsome recompense.'

Late at night two tough-guy types did indeed turn up. It seemed the hairy Prince P— had gambling debts. 'Out,' Mixed-Up grinned in his sweetest way. The tough-guy types nodded, slowly. They had long hair and thick lips like Mick Jagger's. 'He's a busy gent. We should of made an appointment,' said the first type to the second. 'Didn't I tell you we should of called?'

'You did,' agreed the second type. 'Got to do these things right, you said, he's royalty. And you was right, my son, I put my hand up, I was dead wrong. I put my hand up to that.'

'Let's leave our card,' said the first type. 'Then he'll know to expect us.'

'Ideal,' said the second type, and smashed his fist into old Mixed-Up's mouth. 'You tell him,' the second type said, and struck the old man in the eye. 'When he's in. You mention it.'

He had locked the front door after that; but much later,

well after midnight, there was a hammering. Mixed-Up called out, 'Who?'

'We are close friends of the Maharaja of B—' said a voice. 'No, I tell a lie. Acquaintances.'

'He calls upon a lady of our acquaintance,' said a second voice. 'To be precise.'

'It is in that connection that we crave audience,' said the first voice.

'Gone,' said Mecir. 'Jet plane. Gone.'

There was a silence. Then the second voice said, 'Can't be in the jet set if you never jump on a jet, eh? Biarritz, Monte, all of that.'

'Be sure and let His Highness know', said the first voice, 'that we eagerly await his return.'

'With regard to our mutual friend,' said the second voice. 'Eagerly.'

WHAT DOES THE *poor bewildered opponent do?* The words from the chess book popped unbidden into my head. *How can he defend everything at once? Where will the blow fall? Watch Mecir keep Najdorf on the run, as he shifts the attack from side to side!*

Mixed-Up returned to his lounge and on this occasion, even though there had been no use of force, he began to weep. After a time he took the elevator up to the fourth floor and whispered through our letterbox to Certainly-Mary sleeping on her mat.

'I didn't want to wake Sahib,' Mary said. 'You know his

trouble, na? And Begum Sahiba is so tired at end of the day. So now you tell, baba, what to do?'

What did she expect me to come up with? I was sixteen years old. 'Mixed-Up must call the police,' I unoriginally offered.

'No, no, baba,' said Certainly-Mary emphatically. 'If the courter makes a scandal for Maharaja-log, then in the end it is the courter only who will be out on his ear.' I had no other ideas. I stood before them feeling like a fool, while they both turned upon me their frightened, supplicant eyes.

'Go to sleep,' I said. 'We'll think about it in the morning.' *The first pair of thugs were tacticians*, I was thinking. *They were troublesome to meet. But the second pair were scarier; they were strategists. They threatened to threaten.*

NOTHING HAPPENED IN the morning, and the sky was clear. It was almost impossible to believe in fists, and menacing voices at the door. During the course of the day both Maharajas visited the porter's lounge and stuck five-pound notes in Mixed-Up's waistcoat pocket. 'Held the fort, good man,' said Prince P—, and the Maharaja of B— echoed those sentiments: 'Spot on. All handled now, achha? Problem over.'

The three of us – Aya Mary, her courter, and me – held a council of war that afternoon and decided that no further action was necessary. The hall porter was the front line in any such situation, I argued, and the front line had held.

And now the risks were past. Assurances had been given. End of story.

'End of story,' repeated Certainly-Mary doubtfully, but then, seeking to reassure Mecir, she brightened. 'Correct,' she said. 'Most certainly! All-done, finis.' She slapped her hands against each other for emphasis. She asked Mixed-Up if he wanted a game of chess; but for once the courter didn't want to play.

10

AFTER THAT I was distracted, for a time, from the story of Mixed-Up and Certainly-Mary by violence nearer home.

My middle sister Muneeza, now eleven, was entering her delinquent phase a little early. She was the true inheritor of my father's black rage, and when she lost control it was terrible to behold. That summer she seemed to pick fights with my father on purpose; seemed prepared, at her young age, to test her strength against his. (I intervened in her rows with Abba only once, in the kitchen. She grabbed the kitchen scissors and flung them at me. They cut me on the thigh. After that I kept my distance.)

As I witnessed their wars I felt myself coming unstuck from the idea of family itself. I looked at my screaming sister and thought how brilliantly self-destructive she was, how triumphantly she was ruining her relations with the people she needed most.

And I looked at my choleric, face-pulling father and

thought about British citizenship. My existing Indian passport permitted me to travel only to a very few countries,
which were carefully listed on the second right-hand page.
But I might soon have a British passport and then, by hook
or by crook, I would get away from him. I would not have
this face-pulling in my life.

At sixteen, you still think you can escape from your
father. You aren't listening to his voice speaking through
your mouth, you don't see how your gestures already mirror his; you don't see him in the way you hold your body,
in the way you sign your name. You don't hear his whisper
in your blood.

ON THE DAY I have to tell you about, my two-year-old sister Chhoti Scheherazade, Little Scare-zade, started crying
as she often did during one of our family rows. Amma and
Aya Mary loaded her into her push-chair and made a rapid
getaway. They pushed her to Kensington Square and then
sat on the grass, turned Scheherazade loose and made phil-
osophical remarks while she tired herself out. Finally, she
fell asleep, and they made their way home in the fading
light of the evening. Outside Waverley House they were
approached by two well-turned-out young men with Beatle
haircuts and the buttoned-up, collarless jackets made pop-
ular by the band. The first of these young men asked my
mother, very politely, if she might be the Maharani of B—.

'No,' my mother answered, flattered.

'Oh, but you are, madam,' said the second Beatle,

equally politely. 'For you are heading for Waverley House and that is the Maharaja's place of residence.'

'No, no,' my mother said, still blushing with pleasure. 'We are a different Indian family.'

'Quite so,' the first Beatle nodded understandingly, and then, to my mother's great surprise, placed a finger alongside his nose, and winked. 'Incognito, eh. Mum's the word.'

'Now excuse us,' my mother said, losing patience. 'We are not the ladies you seek.'

The second Beatle tapped a foot lightly against a wheel of the push-chair. 'Your husband seeks ladies, madam, were you aware of that fact? Yes, he does. Most assiduously, may I add.'

'Too assiduously,' said the first Beatle, his face darkening.

'I tell you I am not the Maharani Begum,' my mother said, growing suddenly alarmed. 'Her business is not my business. Kindly let me pass.'

The second Beatle stepped closer to her. She could feel his breath, which was minty. 'One of the ladies he sought out was our ward, as you might say,' he explained. 'That would be the term. Under our protection, you follow. Us, therefore, being responsible for her welfare.'

'Your husband', said the first Beatle, showing his teeth in a frightening way, and raising his voice one notch, 'damaged the goods. Do you hear me, Queenie? He damaged the fucking goods.'

'Mistaken identity, fleas,' said Certainly-Mary. 'Many Indian residents in Waverley House. We are decent ladies; *fleas.*'

The second Beatle had taken out something from an inside pocket. A blade caught the light. 'Fucking wogs,' he said. 'You fucking come over here, you don't fucking know how to fucking behave. Why don't you fucking fuck off to fucking Wogistan? Fuck your fucking wog arses. Now then,' he added in a quiet voice, holding up the knife, 'unbutton your blouses.'

JUST THEN A loud noise emanated from the doorway of Waverley House. The two women and the two men turned to look, and out came Mixed-Up, yelling at the top of his voice and windmilling his arms like a mad old loon.

'Hullo,' said the Beatle with the knife, looking amused. 'Who's this, then? Oh oh fucking seven?'

Mixed-Up was trying to speak, he was in a mighty agony of effort, but all that was coming out of his mouth was raw, unshaped noise. Scheherazade woke up and joined in. The two Beatles looked displeased. But then something happened inside old Mixed-Up; something popped, and in a great rush he gabbled, 'Sirs sirs no sirs these not B— women sirs B— women upstairs on floor three sirs Maharaja of B— also sirs God's truth mother's grave swear.'

It was the longest sentence he had spoken since the stroke that had broken his tongue long ago.

And what with his torrent and Scheherazade's squalls there were suddenly heads poking out from doorways, attention was being paid, and the two Beatles nodded gravely. 'Honest mistake,' the first of them said apologetically to my mother, and actually bowed from the waist. 'Could happen to anyone,' the knife-man added, ruefully. They turned and began to walk quickly away. As they passed Mecir, however, they paused. 'I know you, though,' said the knife-man. '"*Jet plane. Gone.*"' He made a short movement of the arm, and then Mixed-Up the courter was lying on the pavement with blood leaking from a wound in his stomach. 'All okay now,' he gasped, and passed out.

II

HE WAS ON the road to recovery by Christmas; my mother's letter to the landlords, in which she called him a 'knight in shining armour', ensured that he was well looked after, and his job was kept open for him. He continued to live in his little ground-floor cubby-hole, while the hall porter's duties were carried out by shift-duty staff. 'Nothing but the best for our very own hero,' the landlords assured my mother in their reply.

The two Maharajas and their retinues had moved out before I came home for the Christmas holidays, so we had no further visits from the Beatles or the Rolling Stones. Certainly-Mary spent as much time as she could with Mecir; but it was the look of my old Aya that worried

me more than poor Mixed-Up. She looked older, and pow-
dery, as if she might crumble away at any moment into dust.

'We didn't want to worry you at school,' my mother
said. 'She has been having heart trouble. Palpitations. Not
all the time, but.'

Mary's health problems had sobered up the whole family. Muneeza's tantrums had stopped, and even my father
was making an effort. They had put up a Christmas tree in
the sitting-room and decorated it with all sorts of baubles.
It was so odd to see a Christmas tree at our place that I
realised things must be fairly serious.

On Christmas Eve my mother suggested that Mary
might like it if we all sang some carols. Amma had made
song-sheets, six copies, by hand. When we did O *come, all
ye faithful* I showed off by singing from memory in Latin.
Everybody behaved perfectly. When Muneeza suggested
that we should try *Swinging on a Star* or *I Wanna Hold Your
Hand* instead of this boring stuff, she wasn't really being
serious. So this is family life, I thought. This is it.

But we were only play-acting.

A FEW WEEKS earlier, at school, I'd come across an American boy, the star of the school's Rugby football team,
crying in the Chapel cloisters. I asked him what the matter
was and he told me that President Kennedy had been
assassinated. 'I don't believe you,' I said, but I could see
that it was true. The football star sobbed and sobbed. I
took his hand.

'When the President dies, the nation is orphaned,' he eventually said, broken-heartedly parroting a piece of cracker-barrel wisdom he'd probably heard on Voice of America.

'I know how you feel,' I lied. 'My father just died, too.'

MARY'S HEART TROUBLE turned out to be a mystery; unpredictably, it came and went. She was subjected to all sorts of tests during the next six months, but each time the doctors ended up by shaking their heads: they couldn't find anything wrong with her. Physically, she was right as rain; except that there were these periods when her heart kicked and bucked in her chest like the wild horses in *The Misfits*, the ones whose roping and tying made Marilyn Monroe so mad.

Mecir went back to work in the spring, but his experience had knocked the stuffing out of him. He was slower to smile, duller of eye, more inward. Mary, too, had turned in upon herself. They still met for tea, crumpets and *The Flintstones*, but something was no longer quite right.

At the beginning of the summer Mary made an announcement.

'I know what is wrong with me,' she told my parents, out of the blue, 'I need to go home.'

'But, Aya,' my mother argued, 'homesickness is not a real disease.'

'God knows for what-all we came over to this country,' Mary said. 'But I can no longer stay. No. Certainly not.' Her determination was absolute.

So it was England that was breaking her heart, breaking it by not being India. London was killing her, by not being Bombay. And Mixed-Up? I wondered. Was the courter killing her, too, because he was no longer himself? Or was it that her heart, roped by two different loves, was being pulled both East and West, whinnying and rearing, like those movie horses being yanked this way by Clark Gable and that way by Montgomery Clift, and she knew that to live she would have to choose?

'I must go,' said Certainly-Mary. 'Yes, certainly. *Bas*. Enough.'

THAT SUMMER, THE summer of '64, I turned seventeen. Chandni went back to India. Durré's Polish friend Rozalia informed me over a sandwich in Oxford Street that she was getting engaged to a 'real man', so I could forget about seeing her again, because this Zbigniew was the jealous type. Roy Orbison sang *It's Over* in my ears as I walked away to the Tube, but the truth was that nothing had really begun.

Certainly-Mary left us in mid-July. My father bought her a one-way ticket to Bombay, and that last morning was heavy with the pain of ending. When we took her bags down to the car, Mecir the hall porter was nowhere to be seen. Mary did not knock on the door of his lounge, but walked straight out through the freshly polished oak-panelled lobby, whose mirrors and brasses were sparkling brightly; she climbed into the back seat of our Ford Zodiac and sat there stiffly with her carry-on grip on her lap,

So it was England that was breaking her heart, breaking it by not being India

staring straight ahead. I had known and loved her all my life. *Never mind your damned courter*, I wanted to shout at her, *what about me?*

AS IT HAPPENED, she was right about the homesickness. After her return to Bombay, she never had a day's heart trouble again; and, as the letter from her niece Stella confirmed, at ninety-one she was still going strong.

Soon after she left, my father told us he had decided to 'shift location' to Pakistan. As usual, there were no discussions, no explanations, just the simple fiat. He gave up the lease on the flat in Waverley House at the end of the summer holidays, and they all went off to Karachi, while I went back to school.

I became a British citizen that year. I was one of the lucky ones, I guess, because in spite of that chess game I had the Dodo on my side. And the passport did, in many ways, set me free. It allowed me to come and go, to make choices that were not the ones my father would have wished. But I, too, have ropes around my neck, I have them to this day, pulling me this way and that, East and West, the nooses tightening, commanding, *choose, choose.*

I buck, I snort, I whinny, I rear, I kick. Ropes, I do not choose between you. Lassoes, lariats, I choose neither of you, and both. Do you hear? I refuse to choose.

A YEAR OR SO after we moved out I was in the area and dropped in at Waverley House to see how the old courter was doing. Maybe, I thought, we could have a game of chess, and he could beat me to a pulp. The lobby was empty, so I knocked on the door of his little lounge. A stranger answered.

'Where's Mixed-Up?' I cried, taken by surprise. I apologised at once, embarrassed. 'Mr Mecir, I meant, the porter.'

'I'm the porter, sir,' the man said. 'I don't know anything about any mix-up.'

Acknowledgments

IN 'THE COURTER', the author wishes to thank the following sources for permission to quote material: Buddy Kaye, Ethel Lee and David Hill for lyrics from 'Speedy Gonzales' copyright © 1962, copyright renewed 1990. International copyright secured. All rights reserved. Also © David Hess Music Co. (⅓rd). By permission of Memory Lane Music Ltd. Lyric reproduction of 'Speedy Gonzales' by kind permission of Carlin Music Corp., UK administrator.

'Jambalaya (On the Bayou)', words and music by Hank Williams © copyright 1951 renewed 1980 Acuff-Rose Music Incorporated, USA. Acuff-Rose Opryland Music Limited, London W1. Reproduced by permission of Music Sales Ltd. All rights reserved. International copyright secured.

'Big Girls Don't Cry' (words and music by Bob Crewe and Bob Gaudio) and 'Sherry' (words and music by Bob Gaudio) © 1962, Claridge Music Inc., USA. Reproduced by permission of Ardmore & Beechwood Ltd, London WC2H 0EA.

The passage quoted on pages 66–7 is in fact an account of a game between S. Reshevsky and M. Najdorf, played in 1957 and described in *The Most Instructive Games of Chess Ever Played*, by Irving Chernev (Faber and Faber, 1966).

© Beowulf Sheehan 2015

SIR SALMAN RUSHDIE was born in Mumbai, on the eve of India's Independence, and was educated in England. After graduating from Cambridge University he worked as an advertising copywriter in London before becoming a full-time author.

He is the author of twelve novels, four works of non-fiction and one book of stories. He is the recipient of many prizes and honours including the 'Booker of Bookers' for *Midnight's Children* – the best novel to have won the Booker Prize.

He is a Fellow of the Royal Society of Literature and Commandeur de l'Ordre des Arts et des Lettres. In 2007 he received a knighthood in the Queen's Birthday Honours. He lives primarily in New York.

RECOMMENDED BOOKS BY SALMAN RUSHDIE:

Shame
Imaginary Homelands
East, West

What do we mean by Home?

Love
JEANETTE WINTERSON

VINTAGE MINIS

Liberty
VIRGINIA WOOLF

VINTAGE MINIS

Race
TONI MORRISON

VINTAGE MINIS

Sisters
LOUISA MAY ALCOTT

VINTAGE MINIS

VINTAGE MINIS

The Vintage Minis bring you the world's greatest writers on the experiences that make us human. These stylish, entertaining little books explore the whole spectrum of life – from birth to death, and everything in between. Which means there's something here for everyone, whatever your story.

vintageminis.co.uk